Life -
And How To Get Through It
Without Getting Hurt

To MARTHA
BEST WISHES,
Pat

To Ellen

Introduction

I have lived on this earth now for nearly 70 years, which amounts to approximately 25,550 days. That may not qualify me as an expert on life, but it definitely makes me experienced. Based on that experience, I decided to sit down one day and write about what I have observed and learned over the course of my lifetime.

These observations are not necessarily earth-shattering nor significant with regard to the major issues in the world. They are merely everyday topics that I have found to be of interest to many people. Okay, they are topics which are of interest to me. I have no idea whether or not you will find them interesting.

They deal with topics which I have observed first-hand and in most cases have learned invaluable lessons as a result. I have attempted to pass on those observations and what I have learned from them in this book. They range from things like marriage, parenthood, religion and politics to holidays, college life, pet peeves and deer crossings.

Most of the stories are meant to be humorous, and we all know that humor is a fickle thing. I have told the same joke to several people. Some of them laugh until tears roll from their eyes while others don't crack a smile. After all, jokes are meant to be fun, unless you dwell on ones that include severed animal parts or missing organs. Those tend to get old after four or five times.

Hopefully, you will find these stories interesting, maybe even enlightening. And if nothing else, at least amusing. Don't worry, there is no mention of severed animal parts or missing organs. I'm saving that for my next book.

Life - And How To Get Through It Without Getting Hurt

Doctor Appointments

Having to go the doctor is not something one looks forward to since it usually means a person is ill or injured and in need of some sort of medical attention. It's expensive, time-consuming and extremely annoying. Here's how it works.

First you call the doctor's office to schedule an appointment. The receptionist answering your call will put you on hold, telling you they are busy with other patients. Forty-five minutes later, the receptionist will get back to you. After scheduling the appointment, he or she will tell you to make sure to get there twenty minutes ahead of time in order to fill out some forms.

When you arrive at the doctor's office for your scheduled appointment, there will be anywhere from fifteen to thirty people in the waiting room, all with expressions on their faces indicating they have been there for a long time.

When you get to the front desk, the receptionist will hand you a stack of forms and a clipboard and tell you to have a seat and fill out the information. The forms will include everything from your name, address and insurance company to listing your history of illnesses, to whether you have ever been a member of the Communist party.

Twenty minutes later, after having filled out the paperwork, you notice that the same people you saw when you walked in are still sitting there. You hand over the forms to the receptionist and ask how long it will be before you see the doctor. He or she will reply, "Soon."

Eventually, after having fallen asleep in your chair, you are awakened by the receptionist calling your name. He or she will tell you to go down the hall and walk into the third room on the right where you wait another twenty minutes before a nurse comes in to take your temperature and blood pressure. When she leaves, she will tell you the doctor will be in "Soon."

Finally, a doctor comes into the room and begins looking through the forms you were given to fill out. After finishing, he will say, "So, why are you here today?" even though the forms clearly indicate the reason why.

After checking your heart rate, looking in your eyes, ears and mouth, the doctor will write down something on a piece of paper, hand it to you and tell you to have the prescription filled out at the nearest pharmacy. He will then say something like, "If you experience any side effects, stop taking the medication immediately."

"Side effects? Like what?"

"Upset stomach, dizziness, heart palpitations, shortness of breath, and in rare cases, death."

"One of the side effects is death?"

"Only in rare cases."

You then go back to the front desk, write out

a check, hand it to the receptionist and walk out to your car with a prescription in hand, not knowing what it is, what it's supposed to cure or how long you should take it. The only thing you know for sure is that if death occurs, stop taking the medication immediately.

Inventions

Throughout the course of history, man has thought of ways to make our lives better. They are called *inventions*. From the wheel to the electric light bulb to the computer, we have been able to continually advance as a society thanks to men and women of intelligence, foresight and ingenuity.

The benchmark for inventions is obviously sliced bread. I know this to be true because each time someone invents something, it is referred to as the "greatest thing since sliced bread."

Speaking of bread, did you know that the Earl of Sandwich was credited for having invented the sandwich? How much thought had to go into that? What did he do, go into his laboratory, place a piece of bread on top of another piece of bread, then place a piece of meat on top and write in his diary, "I feel like I'm really getting close?"

When listing the greatest inventions, most would say the automobile, the telephone and the computer. For me, my favorite inventions are ones that make my life simpler.

For example, at the top of my list would be fast food drive-throughs. When McDonalds first came up with the idea of pre-cooked burgers and fries, you still had to get out of your car, walk up to the window, place your order, and then walk back to your car with your food.

Granted, it only took 30 seconds. But when they invented the drive-through it became even easier. You pull up to the window in your car, place your order, give them your money and within seconds you're driving off with a sack of food that was prepared somewhere between an hour ago and last Tuesday.

Next on my list of greatest inventions is the TV remote control. Remember when you would be in the middle of watching a show and suddenly an ad came on for some kind of feminine hygiene product and you were forced to sit there and watch it? Thanks to the TV remote, those days are gone. Now all you have to do is change the channel with one press of a button, count to sixty and go back to watching your show.

A close third on my list is the weather channel. Talk about brilliant inventions. You can actually turn on TV and get not only the forecast for the next 24 hours but for the next five days.

Plus, they've added a feature which includes an hourly forecast. Which means if you're watching a big game on TV and the hourly forecast indicates its not going to rain for two hours, you get to finish watching the game before mowing the lawn.

Sometimes they don't get it right. On average, I would say the hourly forecast is wrong approximately 50 percent of the time, the 24 hour forecast 75 percent of the time and the five day forecast 100 percent of the time.

Still, with all the latest technology at their disposal, it's good to know what the weather experts predict is going to happen. If I look out my window and see black clouds approaching with rumbles of thunder in the distance, I can take comfort in knowing that according to the forecast it's going to be partly cloudy for the rest of the day with a zero percent chance of precipitation.

Assembly Required

I will be the first to admit that I am not very handy when it comes to putting things together. If I need to purchase an item at a store, say a kid's bike, and I see the words, *"Some assembly required,"* I will immediately break into a cold sweat and curl up in a fetal position on the floor.

A big part of my problem with assembling things is that I hate reading the instruction manual. It's usually long, complicated and printed in the smallest font size possible. Somewhere around page 70, there will be an instruction that reads, *"Attach sections D and F by placing sections B and E at a 45 degree angle and inserting hex nuts J in the designated holes shown on page 45 using a size three-eighth inch Allen wrench.*

Whenever possible, I offer to either purchase the floor model or pay an extra 50 bucks to have someone at the store assemble it. Otherwise, I'm stuck with having to do it myself at home, and the results aren't usually pretty.

I have purchased a kids swing set that came in a box no bigger than an average size suitcase. It took me two weeks to put it together and when it was finally finished the kids thought it was a jungle gym.

I have purchased an outdoor gas grill that came in 240 pieces, not including the nuts and bolts. It works fine as long as you place the meat below the wheels and use a wire and jumper cables to ignite the burner.

I have learned the hard way *never* to attempt to to install or fix anything that involves plumbing or electricity. I have set outlets on fire and have flooded the bathroom while trying to execute seemingly simple tasks. I have blown fuses which have cut the power to not only our house but the entire neighborhood, set the lawnmower on fire, and once nearly electrocuted my wife.

After years of failure, I have finally reached the conclusion that I am not a very handy person. In fact, I'm probably considered a danger to myself and loved ones. Therefore, I have limited my handyman tasks to changing light bulbs. Anything beyond that will result in picking up the phone and calling someone who knows what they're doing.

Holidays

Over the course of time, society has developed and maintained certain customs and celebrated certain events which have become traditional. We call them *holidays*. We tend to take these for granted and go along with them. But if one were to sit down and really ponder them, many would seem unnecessary and some even bordering on stupid.

I decided to sit down one day and make a list of our national holidays and why we celebrate them. I put them into two categories, those that make sense, and those that we can do without.

The first one, of course, is *New Year's Day*

which appropriately falls on January 1st. I can live with that one I suppose. It doesn't make a whole lot of sense to celebrate a day simply because it's the first day of a new calendar year, but what the hell, it's an excuse for consuming large quantities of alcohol the night before and laying on the couch the next day wishing you were dead.

Next up on the calendar are *Martin Luther King Day* and *President's Day*. I lumped them together because they are similar in that they honor our great leaders of the past. No problem there.

The next one is *Easter*, which I do have some problems with. First of all, it falls on a Sunday which most working people have off anyway, so it's kind of a waste of a holiday. Plus, the idea of celebrating Jesus rising from his tomb and ascending into heaven has nothing to do whatsoever with filling baskets with candy and hiding eggs in the backyard.

Then comes *Mother's Day*, which has always confused me and always will because I have no idea exactly what the day is supposed to celebrate. For the first 21 years of my life I thought it was a day to honor my mother by being nice to her and getting her a card and some flowers. But then I got married and started having kids and learned the hard way that it wasn't a day for honoring *my* mother. It was a day for honoring *all* mothers, which included my wife, who I ignored by spending the day with my mom. That was a mistake that I'm still paying for to this day.

Which brings us to *Memorial Day*, which is meant to be a day for honoring those who served in the military and are now deceased. But we all know that it's main function is to usher in the unofficial start of summer. It's the first day off for most working people in months and we celebrate it by loading up the car and traveling somewhere with the family, usually to places like Mount Rushmore or the Ozarks.

Next comes *Father's Day*, which is a totally made-up holiday that's supposed to compensate for Mother's Day. If one were to ask fathers what they would wish for most on Father's Day, 90 percent would say to get rid of Father's Day - and Mother's Day. Basically it's a day where dads get to sit around and not feel guilty about not mowing the lawn, and thanking family members for the ties that we will never wear.

Finally a real holiday occurs every July 4th called *Independence Day*. This one qualifies as a legitimate, in your face, full-fledged holiday that every American, young and old can celebrate. Independence Day has it all - parades, band concerts, barbeques, alcohol and fireworks. There's nothing that says *America* like drinking a 12-pack of beer and setting off explosives in the dark with your kids standing next to you.

That's followed by *Labor Day*, which nobody understands other than it's a day off work. I think it's got something to do with honoring the working class people, but everyone knows it simply as the last holiday of summer and one more opportunity to load up the car and take the family to Mount Rushmore or the Ozarks.

The next one I have a definite problem with - *Columbus Day*. A guy sets sail having no idea where he's going, thinks he lands in India when it's actually San Salvador, calls the natives he meets there *Indians* and heads back to Europe.

And for that we celebrate this idiot's cluelessness with a national holiday? It's like Lewis and Clark saying they discovered Tibet. This holiday is a travesty and should be done away with.

Then there's *Veterans Day* which is sort of like Memorial Day except many of the people we are honoring are still alive. It's not a big deal holiday and many people don't even know what they are celebrating. We can get rid of this one too.

Next up is my personal favorite - *Thanksgiving*, also known as the *last bastion of male chauvinism*. Men get to sit around all day watching football and drinking beer while the women work their butts off preparing a gourmet turkey dinner. After dinner, the women clean up the leftovers and wash dishes while the men continue to drink and watch more football. And the best part of it is we don't have to buy cards or presents. Talk about a perfect holiday!

Last but not least is *Christmas*. It's probably the only holiday where the older you get the less you enjoy it. For kids it's all about Santa Claus and getting presents under the tree on

Christmas morning. For adults, it's intensive labor. It's hanging up lights and decorations, putting up the tree, spending hours finding a parking spot and fighting angry people in the mall searching for that stupid present that your kid is counting on getting or it will ruin his or her Christmas. Add to that the fact that you have to buy a gift for your wife that she will return on December 26th. Totally lost in all this mayhem is the fact that we are supposed to be celebrating the birth of Jesus.

All in all, we've got good holidays, bad holidays and unnecessary holidays. We've come to accept them all in the custom of tradition, but that doesn't mean we need to like them or even keep them going - except Thanksgiving. I don't want to get rid of that one.

Electoral College

As we all know, our country currently consists of a two-party political system, the Republicans and the Democrats. They are elected to congress by a popular vote among the American people. The one exception is the President, who is elected by something called the *Electoral College*.

The Electoral College was created two hundred years ago because popular votes were too difficult to accurately count and were often subject to voter fraud. So congress came up with the idea of selecting a group of people representing each state to decide which candidate would win that state.

The system was later tweaked by assigning electoral votes to each state based on the number of members in the senate and house of representatives. It was determined that whichever candidate won the popular vote would receive *all* of the electoral votes for that state.

Which means that the voters of Florida, for example, could cast 51 percent of the vote for the Republican candidate and 49 percent for the Democratic candidate, resulting in the Republican candidate receiving all 27 of the electoral votes for that state.

And let's say 70 percent of the voters in Illinois cast their vote for the Democratic candidate, resulting in the Democrat receiving all 21 of the electoral votes for Illinois.

If the popular votes were added up for those two states, the Democratic candidate would easily be ahead. However, due to the way the Electoral College works, the Republican candidate would be ahead by a margin of 27-21.

This system is deeply flawed, to say the least. Proponents of the Electoral College have argued that the system works and that the most deserving candidate is elected President. They would be wrong.

In the 2016 election, Hillary Clinton received 51 percent of the popular vote and yet Donald Trump occupies the Oval Office. Want to hear something even scarier? Only 51 percent of eligible voters went to the polls that year, which means Trump was elected by *25 percent* of eligible American voters.

Unlike 200 years ago, we are now able to accurately count each popular vote in a presidential election. So why do we continue to use the antiquated Electoral College system rather than simply adding up the popular vote? What's wrong with the principle of *"one man, one vote"?* That's how we're supposed to determine things in a democracy, right?

Our son lives in Louisiana and told us he didn't bother to vote for Hillary Clinton because his vote meant nothing. Unfortunately, he's right. Louisiana has voted Republican in the last five presidential elections, including 2016. Anyone voting for the Democratic candidate is wasting their time since all of the 8 electoral votes go to the candidate who receives the majority of the popular vote.

The Electoral College is likely one of the biggest reasons for poor voter turnout in presidential elections. If people don't think their vote counts why bother to vote? There is no reason to continue to use this outdated system. It needs to be done away with and replaced by the right way of electing a candidate - *One man (or woman), one vote.*

First Moon Landing

One of the greatest moments in our history came on July 20th, 1969, when astronaut Neil Armstrong became the first man to walk on the moon. Along with Astronaut Buzz Aldrin, who followed Armstrong a few moments later, the two men roamed the moon's surface for several hours before returning to the module.

Armstrong became a legendary hero to all Americans, and will be forever famous for having uttered the immortal words, "One small step for man, one giant leap for mankind."

It occurred to me as I was watching the preview for the upcoming movie, *First Man*, which tells the story of the momentous event, how did they decide who would be the first man to step on the moon and who would be second? Obviously, Armstrong became the more famous of the two since he was the first one to touch foot on the moon. I just wonder how the decision was made, and who made it. Perhaps it might have gone something like this:

Buzz Aldrin: Okay, 60 seconds to lunar module landing. Are you ready?
Neil Armstrong: I think so. I just need to go over my speech one more time.
Buzz: Your speech? Who said you get to make the speech? I thought I was going to do it.
Neil: No, Buzz. We agreed you get to say, The Eagle has landed, and then I step onto the moon's surface and give my speech. We talked about this, remember?
Buzz: You talked about it. I just went along with you so you'd shut up.
Neil: Well, all I know is I'm giving the speech.
Buzz: Oh, yeah? And why's that?
Neil: For one thing, who ever heard of a guy named "Buzz" being the first guy to land on the moon?

Buzz: What's wrong with "Buzz"? I think it's got a ring to it. This is Buzz Aldrin, first man on the moon.
Neil: That's your speech? That's lame, man.
Buzz: Oh yeah, what's yours?
Neil: This is Neil Armstrong, first man on the moon.
Buzz: That's the same as mine, dumb ass. Change yours.
Neil: I'm not changing mine. You change yours.
Buzz: Suppose we arm wrestle for it?
Neil: Are you serious? Arm wrestle? We're wearing 40 pound insulated suits. I can't even bend my arm.
Buzz: Okay, how about paper, rock, scissors?
Neil: You're a moron, you know that? How did you ever make it through flight school?
Buzz: How about this? Whoever thinks up the best speech gets to say it.
Neil: We've got 20 seconds before we land. It took me six months to come up with, This is Neil Armstrong, first man on the moon.
Buzz: Yeah, well I just came up with one off the top of my head.
Neil: Fine. Let's hear it.

Buzz: This is Buzz Aldrin, making a giant leap on the moon for all of mankind.
Neil: It's not a giant leap. It's one small step, man. One small step. Hey, I think I'm onto something.
Buzz: I like giant leap better. It's more symbolic. I win. Let me through. I'm going out.
Neil: Fine. Have it your way. But you better tie your shoe so you don't trip.
Buzz: My shoe? Which shoe? They look fine to me……. hey. where the hell do you think your going? Get back here, you son of a bitch. You better not steal my line.

Men vs. Women

It was Jay Leno who once said, "The difference between men and women is men think the Three Stooges are funny, and women don't." He may have been joking when he said it, but there is a lot of truth behind it. Men and women have different senses of humor. For most men, seeing someone slip on a banana peel will cause them to break out in laughter. Most women will tend to feel sorry for the person and offer to help them.

For whatever reason, men in general find slapstick humor to be funny. The Three Stooges, The Marx Brothers, and Laurel and

Hardy in the old days, Chevy Chase, Will Ferrell and Chris Farley in the modern age. Women in general do not find these people funny. They find them stupid. What they tend to think as funny are things that happen in real life. A baby shampooing his or her hair with oatmeal. A two-year old attempting to eat soup with a fork. A group of six-year olds making a mixture of homemade lemonade and root beer and selling it on the street corner for 25 cents a glass.

Women are far more meticulous and patient than men. If the remote control is missing, I will spend two minutes searching for it before giving up. My wife will spend as much time as necessary before finding it.

Women are content to turn on a show on TV and watch it to its conclusion. Men will channel surf during every commercial to see what else is on.

Men like grill food. Women like casseroles. If Mimi and I walk into a *Steak and Shake* I'm getting a double cheeseburger, fries and chili. She will look over the menu for ten minutes before selecting a grilled cheese sandwich, potato salad and coleslaw.

Men like *guy* movies that include graphic violence and nudity. Women like *chick* movies where they take tissues out of their purses to wipe their tears.

Women like to discuss things, especially following an argument. Men like to forget what happened and move on. Men can't remember what the argument was about after twenty minutes. Women will remember it for years and will often bring it up during the fourth quarter of the Super Bowl.

Women have intuition, men don't. If Mimi seems upset about something and I ask her if something is bothering her, if she says "No" then that means it's nothing I did and I can go back to watching TV. She will stare at me for twenty minutes before finally saying, "Don't you care about me?"

If a man and woman decide to go out for dinner, the man will change his shirt, finish his beer and head toward the garage to get in the car. The woman will go upstairs and be gone for half an hour doing God knows what before coming downstairs and saying, "I'll be ready in ten minutes."

Christmas Spirit

We've all heard the term "Christmas spirit" and now that the season is drawing near I thought it would be appropriate to elaborate on just what "Christmas spirit" really means. For some it's celebrating with family around the Christmas tree and exchanging gifts. For others it's worshipping the birth of Jesus. And for some, it's a reason to give thanks and reach out to those less fortunate by purchasing items and donating them to GoodWill.

For me it's none of the above. My personal take on the holiday season is about finding a parking space at the mall, fighting through lines of angry customers and getting ripped off by paying $75 for a pair of jeans that would normally cost $30.

I've lived through nearly 70 holiday seasons in my lifetime and I can say without hesitation that once I passed the age of seven they all sucked. That was the age when I found out there was no Santa Claus, that it was a hoax perpetrated on young children to believe that one person was capable of delivering presents to every household in the world - in one night.

When I realized that it wasn't Santa who put that bicycle by the tree on Christmas morning, but rather my parents, my world was suddenly shattered. I began doubting things - like the Easter Bunny, the tooth fairy, and even God. If Santa Claus was a hoax, then what was I supposed to believe in?

As I grew older and had kids of my own, I played along with the whole "Christmas spirit" charade for their sake, knowing I was lying through my teeth about Santa and his elves and reindeer.

"How can Santa make all those presents and pass them out to every child in the world?" asked my six-year old son one Christmas Eve.

The logical part of me wanted to answer, "It's not possible, son. I can't believe it took you this long to figure it out." But being a responsible father, with my wife staring at me not to blow it, I instead answered, "Santa has magical powers which he uses once a year to make all the children of the world happy." Then I poured myself another bourbon and chugged it down.

The truth about Christmas is that it's a carefully-crafted ritual predicated on two things, 1) to bring joy and happiness for a 24-hour period to people under the age of eight, and 2) to provide a profit bonanza for every retail store in the free world. For the rest of us, it's a veritable nightmare of hanging lights in zero-degree temperatures, fighting crowds at the mall and buying a stupid tree that you bring into your house for two weeks and hope it doesn't catch on fire.

Then there's the actual ritual of celebrating the holiday, which consists of 4,895 parishioners out of 5,000 attending Christmas mass on Christmas Eve afternoon so they can get it out of the way, opening gifts that aren't remotely close to anything you would ever use or wear and watching your wife open the present you stood two hours in line for say, "Oh, another sweater, just like the one you got me last year."

But, hey, who am I to trash the most time-honored holiday on the yearly calendar? I go along with it, just like every other adult over the age of 30, pretending to act surprised when your son or daughter open that special present they *"secretly"* asked Santa for at the mall two weeks before Christmas. I was a kid once. I remember the feeling. It's just too bad we can't be seven forever.

Soap Operas

The other day I took my car in for service and after taking a seat, I started watching a TV show that happened to be on in the waiting room. It was some sort of soap opera. I had never paid attention to soap operas before but noticed that the other people in the room were riveted to the TV and obviously interested in what was going on. So I decided to pay attention to see what it was about.

After it was over, another one came on which seemed a lot like the one I had just watched but with different characters. It occurred to me that these shows must be popular based on the attention the people in the waiting room were paying to them. So with nothing better to do, I began taking notes and soon came up with my own idea for a soap opera. I even gave it a name - *"The Days of Love, Hate, Sex, Drugs and Revenge."*

The premise centered on David and Nora, a happily married couple living in a nice house in a well-to-do neighborhood. One day when David came home from work, the phone rang. It was a voice saying that Nora had been kidnapped and that David had to pay 1 million dollars ransom. He was told to go to an abandoned parking lot at 8:00 that night with the money, at which point the kidnapper would turn Nora over to David.

Distraught, David took 1 million dollars out of his secret vault in the den and drove to the abandoned parking lot as ordered, where he saw a van which blinked its lights twice. David got out of his car and approached the vehicle, where a man demanded that David hand over the money.

After doing so, a second man got out of the van, opened the back doors and brought out a white poodle. After a moment, David realized the men had kidnapped Nora's dog, whom she named Nora after herself. David tried to get his money back but the van sped off.

David drove home with Nora (the poodle) and found his wife Nora lying unconscious on the kitchen floor. After calling 911, the paramedics showed up at the house and placed Nora on a stretcher and rushed her to the hospital.

Nora slipped in and out of consciousness over the next few days and was only able to mutter the word "Chuck" over and over. The doctor revealed to David that Nora was pregnant.

The next day, a man came into Nora's hospital room. When David asked the man what his name was, he replied, "Chuck." He said he was Nora's partner at the bridge club she attended each week and was worried when she didn't show up.

David told Chuck that Nora had been saying his name repeatedly and asked him why she would do that. Chuck finally broke down and revealed that he and Nora had been carrying on an affair for the past year.

David and Chuck began struggling, with David shoving Chuck against a wall, severing Chuck's spinal cord and leaving him paralyzed. At that moment, Nora woke up and saw Chuck lying on the floor and David standing over him. Nora didn't recognize either man, asking who they were. After diagnosing her, the doctor told David that she displayed the symptoms of amnesia.

Chuck was consigned to a wheelchair, and vowed to seek revenge against David. The following night as David walked to the parking lot to drive home, he was confronted by two men who proceeded to beat him with tire irons, leaving him unconscious.

It turns out that Chuck was a drug dealer, and hired the two men to beat up David. Paramedics found David lying in the parking lot and took him to the emergency room, where doctors performed immediate surgery to remove a blood clot from David's brain.

That's when the service rep came in and told me my car was ready. I saved my notes and am planning to send my manuscript to a Hollywood producer. I'm pretty sure it's a can't miss, sure-fire gem.

Religion

I can say without hesitation that I am a certified Catholic. I was baptized and confirmed. I was an altar boy. I went to church every Sunday, to confession on a regular basis and attended a Catholic school from first grade through high school. Here is what I learned over that 12-year period.

Nuns are some of the meanest people in the world. I have been rapped on the knuckles with a wooden ruler, slapped on the side of the head and smacked with a yardstick. And that was just first grade. I have no recollection to this day what I did to deserve such punishment. But it happened. And I still have the welt marks to prove it.

Nuns believe it is their job to put the fear of God into our brains and to constantly remind us that if we do anything wrong we will burn in hell for eternity. They may think they are teaching us a valuable life lesson, but in reality nuns are basically sadistic bullies with free reign to terrify children into behaving and not breaking any of the ten commandments. Remember Sister Mary Stigmata in the *Blues Brothers*? That was not an exaggeration, folks. That was life in a Catholic school in the 50s and 60s.

The priests weren't much different. They taught religion based on *"Dreading the loss of heaven and the pains of hell."* We had to recite those very words every day during the *Act of Contrition* prayer. They didn't tell us that if we were good we got to go to heaven as much as that if we were bad we would we would suffer eternal damnation. It wasn't a *form* of brainwashing - it was the very definition of brainwashing.

Everything about nuns and priests reeked of morbidness, from the black outfits they wore to the never-changing grim looks on their faces.

Their message was clear - step out of line and suffer the consequences. That's how I was brought up and that's how I pretty much lived for the first 18 years of my life. Then it all changed.

I went off to college in Dubuque, Iowa, which was some 70 miles away from home. For the first time in my life, I was on my own. And boy, did I make the most of it. No one telling me to go church or confession, no one telling me to do my homework or be in bed by 10:00 and up by 7:00. And most importantly, no one hovering over me waiting to punish me for doing something wrong.

I spent the next nine months doing something wrong on virtually a daily basis. Other than killing someone, I may have broken every commandment, although I never did understand what the term *covet* meant, so I'm not sure if I broke any of those.

I stopped going to church on Sundays, stopped going to confession and gradually stopped feeling guilty about it. There were no nuns or priests to torment me and make my life miserable. And my parents were not around to tell me to do my homework instead of hitting the downtown bars with my dorm mates using a fake ID I had made up for me by a senior for ten bucks.

There was a downside to all of this, of course, which consisted of me having spent all the money I earned over summer break by Thanksgiving, and receiving a 1.5 grade average my first semester. For those of you wondering if that's good or bad - it's bad. If only I had attended classes and done some homework. Oh, well.

These days I still consider myself to be Catholic - just not an avid one. I will partake in Christmas and Easter religious activities with my wife and help put up the Christmas tree and hide Easter eggs for the grandkids. But that's about as far as I'm willing to go. If that's good enough to be accepted into heaven I'll gladly take it. Otherwise, I'm going to hell, and according to every nun and and priest who ever taught me, I'm probably not going to enjoy it.

College

Suffice it to say the most turbulent decade in modern history coincided with the wildest, most depraved, irresponsible four years of my life. It was called *college in the sixties*. For me, college was not an institute for higher learning so much as a venue for partying. And when I say *partying*, I'm not talking about proms and outdoor cookouts. I'm talking *Animal House* partying.

It was a time of social unrest, political infighting and cultural revolution. It was Vietnam, Civil Rights, and *Hippies* vs. *Hardhats*. It was race riots, protests, burning draft cards and American flags. It was the

Beatles, Stones, Motown and Woodstock. It was getting high and dropping out. And there I was, 18 years old and right in the middle of it all.

To say I did some illegal things during my college days would be like saying World War Two was a minor skirmish. I purchased and consumed vast quantities of alcohol using a fake ID. I smoked pot, ate at restaurants and ran out without paying, stole grocery and drug store items under my coat, defaced public property and even spent a night in jail due to a panty raid gone bad.

I never considered myself a criminal or even a bad person. I was just a typical college kid having fun. My rationalization was - everybody else was doing it so it couldn't be that bad. Did I mention I was only 18?

My dorm mates invented ideas that became legendary. Such as *borrowing* a garbage can, filling it full of water, leaning it against the senior counselors door and then calling them on the phone saying there was an emergency at the end of the hall. And squirting lighter fluid under their door at 2:00 a.m. and lighting it with a match while yelling "fire" before running back to our room.

Smoke bombs and M-80s would be set off in the hallways, causing the fire alarms to go off on a nightly basis with the fire department arriving moments later. Circuit boxes would be broken into causing the power in the entire dorm to go out. Stairways would be lubricated with motor oil, and hallways with turpentine. Then there was *free pizza night,* where a pizza delivery van would pull into the parking lot in front of the dorm. As soon as the guy walked into the front lobby with a delivery order, someone would go around the back, open up the van door and grab as many pizzas as he could carry.

Many of these pranks were alcohol related. Actually most of them. Okay, 99 percent of them. Like the time when I made a bet with my dorm mates that I could put a pet alligator to sleep by rubbing it's stomach. The alligator, appropriately named *Chopper,* belonged to one of my roommates and was kept in a large fish tank. After securing the wagers, I picked Chopper up by the back of its neck and proceeded to rub its stomach. After a few minutes Chopper's eye began closing.

"See," I proudly announced to the guys in the room. "I win the bet." Then someone said I needed to prove Chopper was really asleep, so I stuck my index finger down its throat, at which point Chopper woke up and clamped down on my finger. I flung Chopper against a wall, breaking its neck while my finger bleed profusely from 10 puncture wounds. My roommate was able to stop the bleeding by wrapping shipping tape tightly around my finger. We gave Chopper a proper burial by flushing it down the toilet.

Eventually, I managed to settle down enough to earn a degree, which technically was the reason for my being there. Although it was the experience of college dorm life which proved invaluable and worth ten diplomas.

Marriage

    I have been happily married to my wife, Mimi, for 48 years and counting. We raised three sons and have seven grandchildren. We are now both retired and loving it. Looking back on the last near half-century, I realize that for all we've been through and as much as we love each other, I can count the things we have in common on one hand.
    It's pretty amazing, really. We can go through a buffet line at a restaurant and no two things on our plate will be the same. Mimi will stop at the fruit and salad section while I bypass her and go directly to the good stuff. By the time we sit down at our table to eat, Mimi's plate will consist of peaches, pears, tomatoes,

carrots, beans, potato salad and coleslaw, while mine will contain chicken, roast beef, pork, ham and french fries.

Mimi likes to read books. I like to watch movies. She hates watching anything that involves monsters, aliens or make-believe characters. She also dislikes silly, slapstick comedies. And even when she does enjoy a movie, she will rarely want to see it again.

I like movies about monsters, aliens and make-believe characters. I also like silly, slapstick comedies and will watch the same movie until I have memorized every line. One of Mimi's most often quoted lines is, "Didn't you just watch that movie the other night?" To which my reply is usually, "Yes. What's your point?"

I like to tell jokes. Mimi not only dislikes most jokes, she doesn't like me to tell jokes. Her idea of funny is when our youngest granddaughter tries to eat peas with a fork. My idea of funny is going through the automatic car wash with Mimi in the passenger seat and rolling down her window during the spray cycle.

When picking out greeting cards for her at a

store I will pick out the first one that says the occasion and has the word *love* in it. She will browse through cards for twenty minutes, reading every word until she finds the perfect one.

Mimi's idea of "getting ready" before guests arrive is to vacuum the carpets in every room, wash the kitchen floor, dust and polish the furniture and thoroughly clean the bathroom. My version is to pick up my underwear off the floor and make sure there's plenty of beer in the fridge.

Needless to say, my wife and I don't have a lot in common. But 48 years is 48 years, and that's got to mean something. Maybe it's the differences that keep us together. At least it keeps things interesting.

Parenthood

In today's society, there are thousands of occupations, career paths and job opportunities one can choose, all which offer formal educational training. Unfortunately, there are no courses that teach a parent how to raise a child. Apparently, that one is up to the parents to figure out on their own. It's sort of the equivalent of learning how to swim by being tossed overboard in the middle of Lake Michigan and having to make it back to shore.

I became a first-time father when I was 22, and figured it was going to be a piece of cake. After all, I was a grown man with a college degree and certainly capable of dealing with someone who couldn't talk, walk, read or write.

What I failed to take into account was that because this person was incapable of performing these fundamental things, he was totally 100 percent dependent on my wife and me. He wasn't going to fix himself a bowl of cereal when he was hungry, or play video games when he was bored, or change his own diaper after pooping.

For those who have never had to deal with baby poop, it's really quite fascinating. It comes in different colors, shapes, sizes, odors and texture. Oh, and it happens a lot.

When the *baby* phase finally passes, its place is taken by the *terrible two* phase. I always thought that was a myth until having to endure it first hand. I didn't think it was humanly possible for a two-year old to inflict that much physical damage and mental cruelty on one's parents.

In truth, raising a child requires having to deal with a continuing number of phases from the time they are born until they are old enough to leave home and set out on their own. And as much as we love our kids, that day can't come soon enough. This phase is known as the *teenage years.*

During this phase, your kids will often turn on you, claiming you don't know what you're talking about and that they are smarter than you. You will also deal with things such as letting them borrow your car and then noticing the next morning on your way to work that the rear view mirror is missing and the transmission will only allow you to go in reverse.

You will also hear the following responses a lot: "I have no idea what you're talking about," "I had nothing to do with it" and "Um, that's not mine." If you have more than one child, (my wife and I had three sons), there will be a lot of fighting between them which involves broken noses and an ample amount of bleeding.

Eventually, everything has a way of working out. Our boys all managed to grow up healthy, happy and successful. And they love us as we have have always loved them. We sit around and laugh about things that used to drive us to the brink of insanity. In short, we not only survived parenthood, we would do it all over again in a heartbeat. Except for the poopy diapers.

Bible Stories

    Growing up in the catholic faith, I was taught early on to read the bible. Actually, I was taught to not only read the bible, but to use it as a guide for how to live my life.
    Reading the bible from beginning to end was difficult, since some of the words were hard to understand, and that the book was the approximate size of Rhode Island. Some of the stories, especially in the old testament, were pretty lame and hard to believe actually happened. Noah's Ark? Come on.
    Eventually as I grew older I realized many of the old testament stories were not to be taken

literally, but were meant as *parables* to explain how God created the world and its inhabitants. Still, the message we were told
from day one was, *if it's in the bible, it must be true.*

With that in mind, I started reflecting one day on some of the more popular old testament stories and the lessons we were supposed to take from them.

There was one story in particular that I remember, and one that I think represents what the old testament was all about. It's the story of the Tower of Babel. I won't bore you with quotes from the book of genesis, but rather provide you with a *Cliff Notes* version.

Around ten thousand B.C. the descendents of Noah were living in a region called Babylon. The population was growing and they all spoke the same language. (This will come into play later on in the story.)

One day a king named Nimrod decided it would be cool to have his people build a tower tall enough to reach heaven.

King Nimrod, being somewhat arrogant, thought that by reaching heaven he would become God-like himself. And so the people went to work building the tower, using bricks and tar for mortar.

After several years, the tower was tall enough to satisfy Nimrod, who proceeded to climb the steps to the very top, bringing with him a large bow and arrow.

When Nimrod reached the top step, he drew his bow and shot an arrow into the sky. Why he chose to do this is unknown, but it most likely was to let God know that he had reached his level and could potentially strike him with an arrow.

This pissed God off, and he proceeded to teach Nimrod a lesson for using poor judgement and bad behavior. Rather than strike Nimrod dead along with all those responsible for building the tower, God chose to have them start speaking different languages.

Why God thought of that as punishment I have no idea. What it did accomplish was mass confusion among the people, who suddenly could not understand what the person next to them was saying.

And so they scattered in all directions, leaving Nimrod standing at the top of the tower holding his bow. Nimrod watched as the people fled, no doubt second guessing his decision to build the tower and fire an arrow toward God.

The result of all of this was the formation of new lands that eventually became countries with their own languages. Fittingly, the tower became known as the Tower of Babel, which we all know is a term used today to describe incoherent noise and confusion.

The odds of the story being completely true are probably one in million, just like Noah's Ark. True or not, it makes for good storytelling. And that's what the old testament writers were good at.

Popular Sayings

Have you ever wondered where often-used terms such as *"Having a chip on your shoulder"* or *"Barking up the wrong tree"* originated? Neither have I. We use phrases and sayings like these frequently, but most of us don't really understand their true meaning or origin.

Some of them are logical, like "A stitch in time saves nine" and "Looking for a needle in a haystack." But there are others that don't seem to make any sense. So, I decided to sit down one day and look up the origins of sayings that people use but probably don't know what they mean or where they came from. (It was either that or mow the lawn.)

For example, the origin of *"Painting the town red"* dates back to 1837, when the Marquis of Waterford led a group of friends on a night of drinking, where they painted doors of homes and several local statues with red paint. Since then, it has come to symbolize a wild night of drinking, especially in town.

"*Three sheets to the wind*" was a term sailors used back in the 18th century to describe a state of drunkenness aboard a ship. The *sheets* were a term for *sails,* and if a sheet was not tied down properly and allowed to float freely in the wind, it usually meant that the sailor responsible was drunk. Three sheets in the wind meant that most of, or all the crew were drunk.

"*Hair of the dog that bit you*" comes from an old English believe that if a person were bitten by a rabid dog, covering the wound with the same dog's hair would cure the person. It has since come to mean that if a person is suffering from a hangover, the cure is to drink the same beverage the next day.

"*Letting the cat out of the bag*" dates back to 16th century England, where suckling pigs were stashed in bags and sold on street corners. Sometimes, the pig would be replaced by a far less valuable cat and put in the bag to be sold to an unsuspecting buyer. If the cat were let out of the bag, it would tip off the buyer and negate the deal.

I could go on, but I heard there was a chance of rain in the forecast, so I better mow the lawn and *"make hay while the sun shines."*

Air Travel

There was a time not so long ago when making a journey from say, Cincinnati to San Francisco would take months by covered wagon. Then, due to the invention of the automobile, that same journey would only take two to three days tops. But thanks to the Wright brothers, such a trip could be accomplished in a few hours.
 The reason I use the term *could* is because along with the invention of the airplane came the necessity to build airports. Thanks to airports, a journey from Cincinnati to San Francisco can vary in time a tad. By a *tad*, I mean anywhere from several hours to a week.

If you think I'm exaggerating, then you've obviously never experienced first-hand a connecting flight through O'Hare International Airport during a snowstorm the week before Christmas. It can range from inconvenient to something out of a Stephen King novel.

The first thing you need to know about large modern-day airports is that they are not merely terminals and runways. They are vast structures the size of major cities consisting of twelve hundred people per square foot.

Before you even actually set foot in an airport terminal there are several steps you must go through. These include finding a parking spot for your car, which is normally located three and a half miles from the main terminal, finding a shuttle bus to take you from the parking lot to the terminal, and standing in a line along with several hundred other people to confirm your plane ticket and check your bags in.

Then you stand in another line where a person will tell you to remove any metal objects from your pockets and take off your shoes

before walking through a scanner which determines if you are carrying a bomb.
Once you have accomplished those things, the next step is finding your gate. This involves having to look at the *arrivals and departures* monitors located throughout the main terminal which display the flight number, brand of airline, destination and gate number.
If you are really, really lucky your gate will be within a reasonable walking distance. Otherwise, you will need to follow signs indicating where your gate is located. Often times this requires hopping on escalators which take you to a train terminal, where you fight several dozen people for a spot that transports you to a different concourse.
Once you have arrived there, you must get on a moving walkway which takes you to the next concourse, where you again hop on an escalator taking you to the next level within the concourse. From there, you will see an endless array of gates, normally with a letter followed by a number. Your gate could be anywhere from a couple hundred feet away to two miles.

Finally, you will arrive at your gate, sometimes the same day you first parked your car in the lot. Once there, you wait in another line in order to board the plane. When you find your seat after stuffing your travel bag in an overhead compartment, you will sit there for an hour before the plane departs the gate.

Then you will sit for another hour on the runway waiting for your plane to take off. That's when the captain gets on the intercom and tells you that due to lightning in the area the plane is not allowed to take off until the weather clears.

At some point later that day or the day following, the captain will tell you that the plane has been cleared for takeoff, but that due to the weather delay there are 27 planes ahead of yours waiting to take off.

Finally, your plane makes it to the main runway and has been cleared for takeoff. Once you are in the air, the captain will apologize for the delay and inform you that the flight will take three hours and twenty minutes. Then you look at your watch and realize it was seven hours ago that you first checked in and that you have no chance of making it to the rehearsal dinner for your daughter's wedding.

Overall, air travel has it's good points and bad. It's usually better than driving, and way better than having to travel in a covered wagon. Well, maybe not *way* better. Let's say it's a toss up.

Movies

I'm a movie fan. I was going to use the word *buff* but I hate that word. If anyone tells me they are interested in or excel at something and they use the word the *buff* I immediately stop listening to anything they have to say.

For me, there are great movies, good movies, average movies and bad movies, and none of them have anything to do with so-called *critically-acclaimed* films. Some of the worst movies I have ever seen have been rated by movie critics as *must-see* films.

That's not to say that *all* critically acclaimed movies are bad. A lot of times they get it right, like *Citizen Kane, Casablanca* and *The Godfather*. But other times they try and sell us on films that are just downright bad, like *The English Patient, Shakespeare in Love* and the worst of them all - *Birdman*. Oh my God, that was an awful movie. For that to have won the Academy Award for best picture is an insult to the motion picture industry. Plus, advertising that it contained full frontal nudity and having it be Ed Norton instead of Naomi Watts was a cruel thing to do to us.

    Which brings me to my point - that movies should be rated on a totally different basis than they are now. First of all, get rid of that stupid star rating. I don't want to know if a movie I'm thinking of watching has one star or four stars. What I want to know is how much I'm going to enjoy it based on the following criteria:

    1) Is it a guy flick or a chick flick?
    2) Is there violence and/or *female* nudity involved?
    3) Are there hidden messages or symbolism that I won't understand?
    4) Is it made by a foreign director who uses subtitles?

5) Are Renee Zellweger, Ben Affleck or Adam Sandler in the movie?

    I want to watch movies that I know ahead of time that I will enjoy, whether its rooting for the good guy to kill the bad guys, laughing non-stop, or having the shit scared out of me. If you saw *The Ring*, then you know that it is one of the most terrifying and disturbing movies of all time despite receiving a below average rating from film critics. I didn't sleep for three nights after watching it and jumped every time the phone rang, refusing to answer it.
    My favorite movies are ones that I can watch over and over again compared to ones that I thought were decent but wouldn't care to watch twice. That should be a definite qualifier for ranking movies. I've seen *A Few Good Men* ("You can't handle the truth") eight times and would watch it again every time it was on, but I wouldn't sit through *The Revenant* more than once even though I thought it was a very good film.
    So, the next time I invest my time and money in going to the theater or renting a

movie I want to know whether I'm going to like it or not. And hearing that it was critically acclaimed or won a bunch of awards isn't the answer. If I'm going to see Ed Norton naked then someone needs to warn me ahead of time. Please.

Sports

Thanks in large part to my dad, I grew up a sports fan. I played football, basketball and baseball throughout grade school and high school and even some in college. I continue to remain an avid fan, particularly of those three sports. But it brings up a question many people have argued over the years - what qualifies as a sport vs. an activity?

Some contend that in order for it to be a sport there has to be ball involved. That would put the *big three* in, as well as soccer, hockey (puck - same thing), tennis and golf. It would also include less popular events such as rugby, volleyball, polo, billiards, table tennis, lacrosse and bowling. However, it eliminates events most consider a sport - boxing, wrestling, swimming, skiing, auto racing, horse racing and all track and field events.

So, clearly, a sport is more than an event which uses a ball. Can it be defined as something in which athletes participate against one another? That certainly broadens the criteria, but would it be limited to events where athletes are in direct competition vs. those where an athlete competes on his or her own and attempts to achieve the best score?

That separates events like football, basketball, baseball, hockey, rugby, tennis, boxing and wrestling from golf, billiards, bowling and any event where an athlete performs before judges and awarded points.

So, the question of what constitutes a sport is obviously one that requires a lot of thought. Fortunately, I have done that and feel qualified to present my own definition. You're welcome.

A sport requires participation between athletes. According to the dictionary definition, an athlete is "*a person who is trained or skilled in exercises or games requiring physical agility, strength or stamina."* Ah, now we're getting somewhere. I think we can immediately eliminate bowlers, jockeys, race car drivers, billiards players, Polo players, chess players, table tennis players and half of all winter olympic competitors. Sorry, guys, but hopping in a bobsled and traveling down a pre-designed manufactured track does not qualify you as an athlete, nor your event as a sport.

Now that we've gotten those out of the way, let's zero in on *real sports* vs. *performance sports*. Real sports have to involve one very important element - an opponent who is trying to stop you from achieving your goal. Figure skating would qualify as a *real* sport only if there were opponents on the ice attempting to take you out. To go out there and perform a routine without anyone getting in your way may require talent, but it's *not* a sport. Same goes with diving, synchronized swimming and gymnastics.

That pretty much leaves only those events that require athletic ability but without an opponent that is trying to stop you. This is

78

where it gets tricky. Professional golf is a great example. Golfers don't compete head-to-head per say, but they do compete against a course which is designed to make their job more difficult. And I believe there is some athletic ability involved. Therefore I would qualify golf as a sport.

Track and field is another tricky one. If you are competing directly against opponents who are attempting to beat you, as in the 100-meter dash, then, yes, put it in the sports category. Same with swimming. However, if you are trying to throw a shot put or a disc farther than the other competitors and there's no one or nothing trying to prevent it, then your event ranks as a performance - but not a sport. I hope that helps clear things up.

World Cup Soccer

Every year I make it a point to try something I have never experienced before. Two years ago it was bungee jumping and last year it was scuba diving. I did not actually participate in either of these events. I simply watched them on television. I may be curious, but I'm not crazy.

This year my goal was to watch World Cup Soccer. Like the Olympics, the World Cup is held every four years and this was a competing year. Having never watched a soccer match in my life, I decided the best way to go into it was to read everything I could regarding the sport, and the World Cup in particular. Here are some of the key things I learned.

The World Cup is officially known as the FIFA World Cup. FIFA stands for the *Federation of International Football Association*. This bothered me since they obviously stole the term *football* from us. I later learned that it was us who stole the term from them. Apparently, soccer is considered football outside the United States.

The next thing I learned was that the USA was not involved in the World Cup. No wonder we don't pay attention to soccer in this country, I thought to myself. FIFA won't let us participate. What a bunch of B.S. that is. Then I found out the USA *is* a member of FIFA and the reason why they aren't in the World Cup is because they lost to both Trinidad and Tobago in the qualifying round. I thought it was unfair that we had to play two matches in order to qualify until I learned that Trinidad and Tobago was one team.

At first I was reluctant to proceed with my plan to watch the World Cup since the U.S. wasn't even in it. But I decided to go ahead and pursue my goal, especially after learning that it is the most widely watched sporting event in the world, even exceeding the Olympics. I was determined to go into this with an open mind and attempt to capture the same excitement for the sport as the millions of fans around the world.

Continuing my research, I learned that 32 teams qualify for the World Cup after the elimination rounds. Teams are selected into eight groups, who play a round-robin tournament with the winner advancing to the next round. Eventually, it comes down to two teams who play for the World Cup final.

I sat down one afternoon and watched my first match between Uruguay and Egypt. My most vivid memory was that for fifteen minutes the two teams kicked the ball around without either goal coming into view. At some point Uruguay managed to kick the ball far enough to awaken the Egyptian goalie, who had apparently fallen asleep.

Unfortunately for Egypt, the ball crossed the goal line and went into the net before the goalie could fully wake up, giving Uruguay a 1-0 lead.

An hour or so later, the referee signaled that the match was over. Final score - Uruguay 1, Egypt 0.

I decided to watch another match the next day between Iran and Morocco, hoping that the Uruguay vs. Egypt match was a fluke and that Iran and Morocco would provide a more exciting offensive match. Three hours later, the match ended. Final score - Iran 1, Morocco 0.

Despite my initial reaction that soccer was the sports equivalent of watching paint dry. I refused to give up. Over the next two days I watched Mexico vs. Germany and Serbia vs. Costa Rica, with both matches ending 1-0. I was convinced that every match ends up 1-0. But I was wrong. The next day Denmark played France, which ended in a 0-0 tie.

I have no doubt that soccer players at that level are great athletes. They run back and forth across an endless field for three hours kicking a ball that either gets intercepted by an opposing player or goes out of bounds, which happens roughly 175 times a match. The end result is - sorry everyone outside the U.S. - boredom on a level I never thought existed in

83

sports, or any other activity that doesn't involve darts, brooms or pushing a potato along the ground with one's nose.

  I heard a few weeks later that France wound up winning the World Cup, which no doubt produced a state of delirium across France. I'm happy for them. I really am. Just like I will be happy for every team that wins the World Cup for as long as it's played. I just won't be watching it.

Traditions

We Americans love to celebrate things. We have our holidays, of course, but apparently there aren't enough of them to satisfy us, so we make up extra ones, most of which are really dumb. Because they're dumb, we can't allow them to be *official* holidays, and so we call them *traditions* instead. Here are some examples:

Groundhog Day - Every February 2nd, a group of people assemble in a small town in Pennsylvania called Punxsutawney, to watch a groundhog come out of its hole. If the groundhog see its shadow that means six more weeks of winter. If it does not see its shadow that means there will be an early spring.

This ritual is lame on so many levels that is actually becomes funny. The reason the groundhog sees its shadow simply means the sun is shining at that moment. If it doesn't see its shadow it's because its cloudy. Here's the best part. *"Studies have shown there is no correlation between the groundhog seeing its shadow and the arrival of spring."* Does that mean there are people out there who thought otherwise?

Valentine's Day - The calendar year just wouldn't complete without devoting a day to express our feelings for someone else. That could easily be accomplished with a simple *"I really like you"*, but no, tradition demands that we purchase greeting cards, flowers and candy, all at jacked-up prices, in order to prove how much we really like that person.

Apparently, if you buy a cheap card and carnations that means you only like that person a little. If you purchase an expensive card and a dozen roses it means you really, really like that person a lot. And if you don't buy anything that means you hate that person and wish they were dead.

If you have passed the *like* phase and moved into the *love* stage, your options require you to spend more money. A lot more money. Dinner at an expensive restaurant is a given. Sorry guys, McDonald's won't cut it - even if you opt to supersize the meal. Jewelry is normally part of the deal, and if you really, really love the person a red sports car will usually put you over the top - until you forget her birthday, which puts you back to square one.

St. Patrick's Day - One day out of each year everyone pretends to be of Irish descent, eats corned beef and cabbage and drinks large quantities of green beer. The day is meant to honor Saint Patrick, who was famous for driving all of the snakes out of Ireland - or was it the protestants? It doesn't really matter, since no one cares about him anymore. They just use his name as an excuse to celebrate something.

April Fool's Day - This is a day when we get

to label those who believe that April 1st is the first day of the calendar year as *fools*. The origin actually dates back to the old Julian calendar, which did in fact regard April as the first month of the new year. It was replaced by the Gregorian calendar in the 17th century, where January 1st is considered the the first day of the new year.

It has become a tradition to celebrate each April 1st by pulling pranks on people, whether they believe it to be the first day of the new year or not. These pranks range from harmless gags, like putting flour in the sugar bowl, to more sophisticated practical jokes, like hiring someone to dress up as a policeman, have them knock on your front door and tell your spouse they have been placed under arrest for embezzlement and tax evasion.

Halloween - Without a doubt the strangest of all the annual traditions, this one deals with both evil spirits and innocent children having fun. Its origin goes back to a pagan ritual where ghosts and goblins roamed the earth on the eve of *All Saints Day*. Over the years it managed to evolve into a night of kids dressing up in costumes and going door-to-door asking people for candy.

Halloween, known as *All Hallows Eve* or *trick or treat night*, depending on one's point of view, ranks as the second most profitable day next to Christmas for the retail industry. Grocery stores sell millions of bags of candy, cookies and suckers while retail stores sell millions of costumes, masks and makeup for the purpose of filling kids' bellies full of useless empty calories, which they vomit out of their systems throughout the night. But, hey, it's all in good fun, right?

Black Friday - The day after Thanksgiving used to be a day to unwind and recover from having consumed pounds of turkey, potatoes, stuffing, yams, broccoli casserole, corn, rolls and pumpkin pie. Not anymore. The day after Thanksgiving has become better known as *Black Friday,* and it's the only day out of the year where shoppers are legally allowed to inflict severe punishment on one another over the purchasing of fifty percent off Christmas items.

Retail stores shamelessly compete for

customers by opening their doors at ridiculous hours, some as early as 8:00 p.m. on Thanksgiving. People line up in droves waiting for the store to open, and then once inside, proceed to maul each other in order to secure the most popular items.

Anyone who falls is immediately trampled upon. Anyone who attempts to wrestle an item away from another customer is kicked and beaten, all in the spirit of the holiday season.

Zombies

For reasons unbeknownst to any adult with an I.Q over 75, zombies have become one of the more popular subjects of books, movies and TV shows over the past decade. I cannot explain this sudden phenomenon but I know it exists. Whenever I go to a movie rental store and look for something to bring home for the family to watch, I see row upon row of films with zombies as the main theme.

Back when I was growing up we had *Dracula, Frankenstein, the Wolfman and the Mummy,* which was all we needed to satisfy our desire for good old fashioned horror. Vampire movies continued to be popular, but have given way to the zombies. There are even TV shows about zombies for kids, for Christ's sake.

Being the open-minded person that I am, I decided to research this zombie craze to see what the appeal was. I started by looking up the definition of zombie in the dictionary. It read, *"The body of a dead person given the semblance of life, but mute and will-less, by a supernatural force, usually for evil purposes."* And children are watching this stuff?

My research then led me to how and when this fascination with zombies began. The origin appears to date back to a 1968 film called *Night of the Living Dead,* which spawned approximately 150,000 imitators like *The Evil Dead, Dawn of the Dead, Day of the Dead* and *Abraham Lincoln vs. the Zombies*. No, that is not a joke. There really is a movie called *Abraham Lincoln vs. the Zombies.* I have not seen it and don't plan to in the near or distant future.

The zombie craze then hit the television industry with shows like, *The Walking Dead, Fear the Walking Dead* and *Ash vs. the*

Walking Dead. Hmmm, there seems to be a common phrase here. If you make a film or TV show with the words *walking* and *dead* in them you're going to make some serious money.

The final phase of my research consisted of actually watching a show about zombies. I got on Netflix and searched on the word *zombie*, which brought up 275 results. I ended up selecting a film called *I, Zombie*, which, from the title alone indicated it had to be about zombies. So I grabbed a beer and some popcorn and sat down to watch it.

The premise revolves around a woman named Sarah and her boyfriend Mark, who travels into the woods one day to collect moss samples when he comes upon an abandoned farmhouse. There he finds a deformed man propped up against a wall. He then hears a woman scream, and upon finding her, notices that she has the same deformities as the man. When he leans down to help her she bites him on his neck and he collapses.

A few weeks later, Sarah calls authorities to report Mark missing. Mark is in the woods killing campers and apparently eating them. He then picks up a hitchhiker and eats him too. He gradually begins to regress, both physically and mentally, and eventually makes his way back to Sarah, who he attacks and - that's as much as I could take. I started channel surfing and lo and behold, came across one of my old favorites - *Frankenstein Meets the Wolfman*. I watched it to its conclusion, loving every minute.

That concluded my research on zombies. Suffice it to say that I am not a fan, nor ever will be - unless they decide to make one with Frankenstein, the Wolfman, Dracula and the Mummy.

Pet Peeves

Everyone has something they don't like in everyday life. It's human nature. If every person was completely happy 100 percent all of the time we would have a society of - happy people, which would be impossible since our political system is designed to prevent that from happening.

Like everyone else, I have everyday things that tend to annoy me. These are commonly known as *pet peeves*. Here are a few examples:

People who still pay for things at stores by writing checks. Come on folks, it's the 21st century for crying out loud. They have these handy little devices that require you to simply swipe your plastic card and you're done. To whip out a check book and a pen is today's equivalent of purchasing a 20-pound sack of flour with a live chicken 200 years ago.

People who come up to you at a party or at your front door and start the conversion by saying, "Hi, my name is Andrew and I would like to talk to you about Jesus."

Receiving telemarketing calls after 6:00 p.m. They are not only annoying, they are an invasion of privacy. If your job is to call random people in the evening to ask 20 survey questions on shoe brands, then please do us all a favor and consider a job at McDonald's instead.

Four-way stops. Four cars pull up to an intersection, stop and stare at each other waiting for the first car to proceed. After approximately two minutes, cars A and B will start out at the exact same moment, causing both to come to a stop. Then cars C and D will do the same thing, causing them to also come to a stop. Then the four cars continue to stare at each other for another two minutes, each having no idea as to who has the right of way. Finally, one car decides to proceed, causing the other three cars to honk angrily. That is followed by the three remaining cars staring at each other waiting for one of them to go until all four cars eventually make it through the intersection.

People who decide to drive in the left lane on an interstate traveling 50 mph, causing a traffic backup and forcing cars to pass in the right lane. Statistics show that the majority of these drivers are men over 65, and they are usually wearing hats.

Deer Crossings

I consider myself knowledgeable regarding the rules of the road. But I have to admit, I don't understand the point of deer crossing signs on interstates and highways. Obviously they are meant to alert us drivers to be on the lookout for deer. I get that part. The part I don't get is what am I supposed to do when there aren't deer crossings signs posted? Since deer can't read, they obviously don't know where they are supposed to cross, which makes it more difficult for the driver.

According to the Department of Transportation, deer crossing signs are posted at areas near where deer tend to populate. To deer, life is one big mass of land that includes trees, crops, fences, creeks, and roads. The only things they are interested in are food, water, shelter and not getting shot by hunters.

So that brings us to the main question - what is my responsibility as a driver with regard to deer? The DOT would say to use caution and look both ways wherever signs are posted. But there's nothing about what I'm supposed to do where signs aren't posted. I consider myself a decent driver, but if I'm traveling from say Des Moines to Chicago there's no way I'm looking for or even thinking about deer the entire trip. If I see a deer crossing sign I will look in both directions and then proceed.

If I happen to hit a deer in a deer crossing area I would feel like it was my fault. However, if a deer runs across a road in front of me outside a deer crossing area I put the blame squarely on the deer. Someone has to take responsibility in that situation and it sure as hell isn't going to be me.

I understand deer are dumb animals incapable of reading road signs. But, they have been nurtured from birth to survive conditions and develop and instinct for staying alive. Therefore, a deer who wanders out of the deer crossing area and decides to run across interstate 80 willy-nilly is taking its life in its own hands (or in this case hoofs) and should be prepared to suffer the consequences.

The DOT claims to receive dozens of phone calls, emails and letters on a monthly basis from people insisting that deer crossing signs be moved to areas where traffic is slower and can avoid hitting the deer. There was even the infamous caller named *Donna* from North Dakota who claimed to have hit three deer over a two-year period at deer crossings on the interstate and insisted to authorities that they be moved to 25-mph speed zones in order to protect both the driver and the deer. While this is of course absurd, it does indicate there are people out there who believe deer should cross only at deer crossings.

All of which brings me back to my original question - what is the responsibility of a driver with regard to deer running across interstates and highways? The only logical answer in my opinion is that motorists have the right of way and deer don't, especially outside deer crossing areas. Sorry, *Bambi*, but you're lower on the food chain list than me. If you want to run across an interstate at 5:00 in the afternoon looking for dinner then you better learn how to dodge traffic.

Epilogue

I certainly hope you have been entertained by these stories, and have not considered them as a personal attack on anyone, regardless of race, color or creed. My only intention was to point out things which I have observed during my lifetime, and look at them from a humorous standpoint. All except for the Electoral College, which I seriously believe to be inept.

I make fun of just about everything else, including myself. I learned a long time ago that I am a flawed person lacking in many areas. Many of these flaws are pointed out by my wife on a daily basis in order to keep me humble. I love her for that, and hope she continues to do so for the rest of our lives together. I realize I am far from perfect, and each time I tend to forget that she reminds me. Thanks, honey.

    The main point of these stories is to make light of everyday situations for the sake of humor. We have plenty of issues in this world to take seriously. Why not balance it out with a few good laughs.

    Anyway, hope you had as much fun reading it as I did writing it.

    Patrick Triplett

Made in the USA
San Bernardino, CA
21 October 2018